How Good can GOD Be?

a story about a little girl
and her daddy

written and illustrated by

Sara Thurman, EdD

Dedication

To my beautiful grandchildren who know just how good God is —
Jonah, Hepzibah, Lilian, Ezekiel, and many more to come.

Grandma loves you in the morning and the evening and all day long.

Your legacy of love and joy is changing the world.

And to all the little-bitty children and all the big-sized children
who read this book, I dedicate this message of love to you, too.

You are all loved children in God's family.
May you experience Father God's love today.

There was once a little girl
who lived on a big, big ranch in Texas
with her family.

When the little girl was a little-bitty girl,
she asked her Daddy,

"How good can God be?"

Her Daddy replied,

"Oh, my daughter,
God is so, so good. God wants to
spend time with you.

Do you want to go with me
and feed the cows?"

The little girl, who was a little-bitty girl exclaimed,

"Yes, Daddy! I want to spend time with you
and feed the cows!"

And together they went in the pickup truck
and put out bales of hay for the cows to eat.

When the little girl was just a little girl,
she asked her Daddy,

"How good can God be?"

Her Daddy said,

"Oh, my daughter,
God is so, so good. God wants to
help you with any task, no matter
how big or how small.

How can I help you today?"

The little girl, who was just a little girl replied,

"Oh, Daddy, can you get the grass burrs
out of the bottoms of my feet?

I wasn't wearing shoes and I got stickers."

And together, they went into the living room.

The little girl sat down and her Daddy very carefully took each sticker out of his little girl's feet.

When the little girl became a medium-sized girl,
she asked her Daddy,

"How good can God be?"

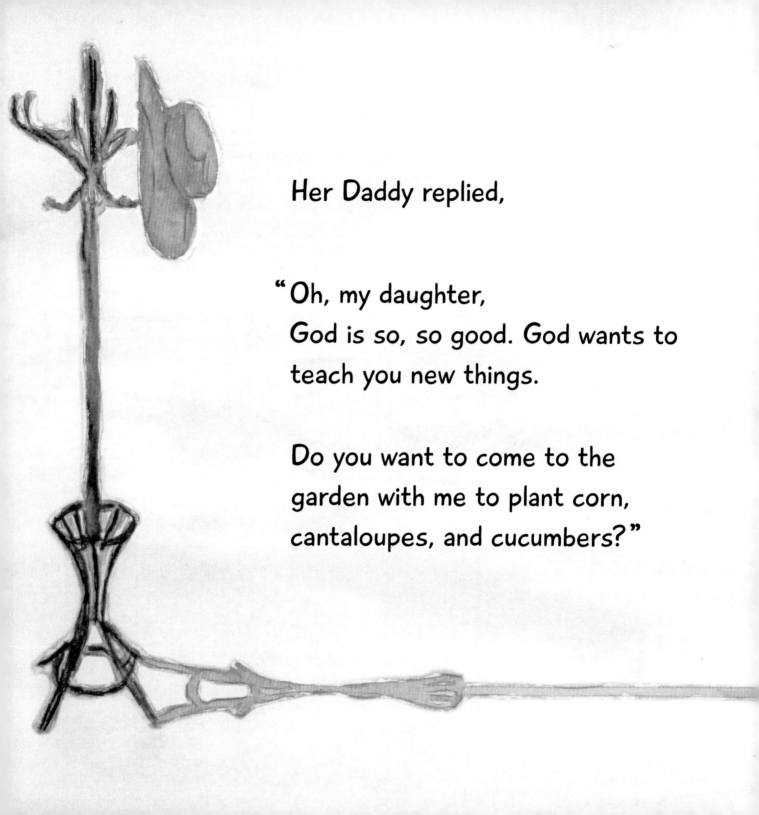

Her Daddy replied,

"Oh, my daughter,
God is so, so good. God wants to
teach you new things.

Do you want to come to the
garden with me to plant corn,
cantaloupes, and cucumbers?"

"Oh yes, Daddy! I want to come learn from you!"
replied the little girl,
who was now a medium-sized girl.

And together,
they planted seeds
in the garden
to become an abundant
harvest some day.

When the little girl became a big-sized girl,
she asked her Daddy,

"How good can God be?"

Her Daddy explained,

"Oh, my daughter,
God is so, so good. God wants to
tell you how much He loves you
and how proud He is of you.

Do you want to come sit with me
and let me tell you just how much
I love you?"

The little girl, who was now a big-sized girl, answered, "Yes!"

And together they sat on the porch.

She listened to her Daddy tell her many, many love stories of how good God can be.

And so if you ever need to know how good God can be,

just ask your Daddy.

He will surely have all the answers.

My Daddy and Mama

Hugh Martin Coston and Olga Sights Coston

Afterword

This story has been in my heart for many years.
My Mama, Olga Sights Coston, gave me the title.

It was her favorite saying in the last years of her earthly life—
"How good can God be?"—more like a factual statement
than a question. She had no doubt of God's goodness.

My earthly Daddy, Hugh Martin Coston, loved me unconditionally
as a little-bitty girl all the way into adulthood. My Daddy spent
time with me, helped me when I needed help, taught me new
things, and told me many, many times how much he loved me.

I was blessed to have a Daddy in my life, a beautiful prototype
of our Heavenly Father who loves us unconditionally
with His time, help, teachings and words.

How Good Can God Be?

I believe each of us has our story to share about the goodness of God.
In my art ministry business, called Acts 1:8 Blessings, I teach and mentor
others to help them discover their story is important, too.

God shows us the importance of our relationships with Him
and with others in our everyday lives. I would love to connect with you.
Follow me and share how good God can be in your own story.

CONNECT WITH ME AT

sarathurman.com

f /actsoneeightblessings   /actsoneeightblessings   /sarathurman58

APPLE PODCAST: Small Beginnings with Sara

Made in United States
North Haven, CT
25 March 2022

17553605R10018